Fish

A Level One Reader

By Cynthia Klingel and Robert B. Noyed

The
Child's
World®

2

Fish can be many colors and sizes.

Fish have gills to breathe underwater.

They have tails and fins to help them swim.

Some pet fish live in a glass bowl.

My fish live in a glass tank. It is called an aquarium.

I feed my fish every day.

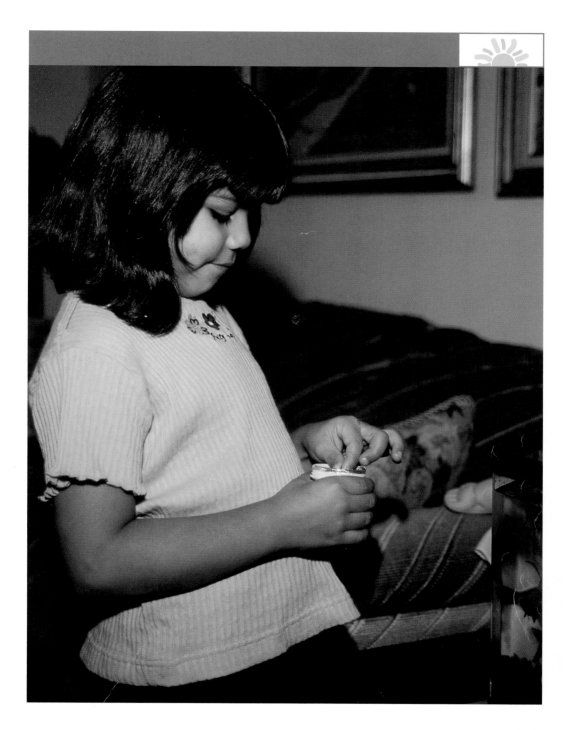

13

14

I sprinkle food on top of the water.

I change the water
every week. This keeps
the aquarium clean.

17

Sometimes I use a net to catch the fish.

Taking care of my fish is fun.

Word List

aquarium

bowl

breathe

fins

gills

tank

underwater

Note to Parents and Educators

Welcome to The Wonders of Reading™! These books provide text at three different levels for beginning readers to practice and strengthen their reading skills. Additionally, the use of nonfiction text provides readers the valuable opportunity to *read to learn*, not just to learn to read.

These leveled readers allow children to choose books at their level of reading confidence and performance. Level One books offer beginning readers simple language, word choice, and sentence structure as well as a word list. Level Two books feature slightly more difficult vocabulary, longer sentences, and longer total text. In the back of each Level Two book are an index and a list of books and Web sites for finding out more information. Level Three books continue to extend word choice and length of text. In the back of each Level Three book are a glossary, an index, and a list of books and Web sites for further research.

State and national standards in reading and language arts emphasize using nonfiction at all levels of reading development. The Wonders of Reading™ fill the historical void in nonfiction material for the primary grade readers with the additional benefit of a leveled text.

About the Authors

Cindy Klingel has worked as a high school English teacher and an elementary teacher. She is currently the curriculum director for a Minnesota school district. Writing children's books is another way for her to continue her passion for sharing the written word with children. Cindy Klingel is a frequent visitor to the children's section of bookstores and enjoys spending time with her many friends, family, and two daughters.

Bob Noyed started his career as a newspaper reporter. Since then, he has worked in communications and public relations for more than fourteen years for a Minnesota school district. He enjoys writing books for children and finds that it brings a different feeling of challenge and accomplishment from other writing projects. He is an avid reader who also enjoys music, theater, traveling, and spending time with his wife, son, and daughter.

Published by The Child's World®, Inc.
PO Box 326
Chanhassen, MN 55317-0326
800-599-READ
www.childsworld.com

With special thanks to Andrea and Elyse Harper,
who provided the modeling for this book.

Photo Credits
© Flanagan Publishing Services/Romie Flanagan: cover, 2, 5, 6, 10, 13, 14, 17, 18, 21
© Nick Dolding/Tony Stone Images: 9

Project Coordination: Editorial Directions, Inc.
Photo Research: Alice K. Flanagan

Library of Congress Cataloging-in-Publication Data
Klingel, Cynthia Fitterer.
Fish / by Cynthia Klingel and Robert B. Noyed.
p. cm. — (Wonder books)
Summary: Illustrations and simple text describe keeping fish as pets in a fish bowl or aquarium.
ISBN 1-56766-799-6 (lib. reinforced)
1. Aquarium fishes—Juvenile literature.   [1. Aquarium fishes. 2. Fishes. 3. Pets.]
I. Noyed, Robert B.   II. Title.   III. Wonder books (Chanhassen, Minn.)

SF457.25 .K58   2000
639.34—dc21   99-057452